For my extended family
—ST

For all who enjoy this special time of year
—CL

Library of Congress Cataloging-in-Publication data is on file with the publisher.

Text copyright © 2019 by Sue Tarsky
Illustrations copyright © 2019 by Claire Lordon
First published in the United States of America in 2019 by Albert Whitman & Company
ISBN 978-0-8075-7729-5 (hardcover)
ISBN 978-0-8075-7723-3 (ebook)

Printed in China
10 9 8 7 6 5 4 3 2 1 WKT 24 23 22 21 20 19

Design by Rick DeMonico

For more information about Albert Whitman & Company,
visit our website at www.albertwhitman.com.

100 Years of Albert Whitman & Company
Celebrate with us in 2019!

Taking a Walk

Fall
in the
Country

Sue Tarsky

illustrated by
Claire Lordon

Albert Whitman & Company
Chicago, Illinois

I went for a walk in the country today.
I saw lots of red, orange, and gold leaves.

They sparkled in the sun and went
crunch on the ground!

I went for a walk in the country today.
I saw sparkling leaves that crunched and
one huge yellow harvest moon.

The moon looked so close I tried to touch it!

I went for a walk in the country today.
I saw sparkling leaves that crunched,
one huge yellow harvest moon,
and two galloping horses.

The horses' hooves went thump-THUMP-thump-THUMP!

I went for a walk in the country today.

I saw sparkling leaves that went crunch,

one huge yellow harvest moon,

two galloping horses, and three little red foxes.

The foxes howled at me!

I went for a walk in the country today.
I saw sparkling leaves that went crunch,
one huge yellow harvest moon,
two galloping horses, three howling red foxes,
and four croaking frogs.

The frogs jumped into a pond when they saw me!

I went for a walk in the country today.
I saw sparkling leaves that went crunch,
one huge yellow harvest moon,
two galloping horses, three howling red foxes,
four jumping frogs, and five digging gray squirrels.

The squirrels were all burying nuts for the winter!

I went for a walk in the country today.
I saw sparkling leaves that went crunch,
one huge yellow harvest moon,
two galloping horses, three howling red foxes,
four jumping frogs, five digging gray squirrels,
and six hares with long ears.

The hares were racing so fast!

I went for a walk in the country today.
I saw sparkling leaves that went crunch,
one huge yellow harvest moon, two galloping horses,
three howling red foxes, four jumping frogs,
five digging gray squirrels, six hares with long ears,
and seven red ladybugs with black spots.

The ladybugs were on plant stems!

I went for a walk in the country today.

I saw sparkling leaves that went crunch,

one huge yellow harvest moon, two galloping horses,

three howling red foxes, four jumping frogs,

five digging gray squirrels, six hares with long ears,

seven red ladybugs with black spots,

and eight shiny red apples.

One apple had a worm coming out of it!

I went for a walk in the country today.
I saw sparkling leaves that went crunch,
one huge yellow harvest moon, two galloping horses,
three howling red foxes, four jumping frogs,
five digging gray squirrels, six hares with long ears,
seven red ladybugs with black spots,
eight shiny red apples, and nine big mushrooms.

The mushrooms looked like little stools!

I went for a walk in the country today.

I saw sparkling leaves that went crunch,

one huge yellow harvest moon, two galloping horses,

three howling red foxes, four jumping frogs,

five digging gray squirrels, six hares with long ears,

seven red ladybugs with black spots,

eight shiny red apples, nine big mushrooms,

and ten geese flying in a V-shape.

The geese all honked at me!

I went for a walk in the country today. I saw

lots of red, orange, and gold leaves

1 huge yellow harvest moon

2 galloping horses

3 howling red foxes

4 jumping frogs

5 digging gray squirrels

6 hares with long ears

7 red ladybugs with black spots

8 shiny red apples

9 big mushrooms

and 10 geese flying in a V-shape.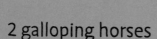

What a good walk I had!

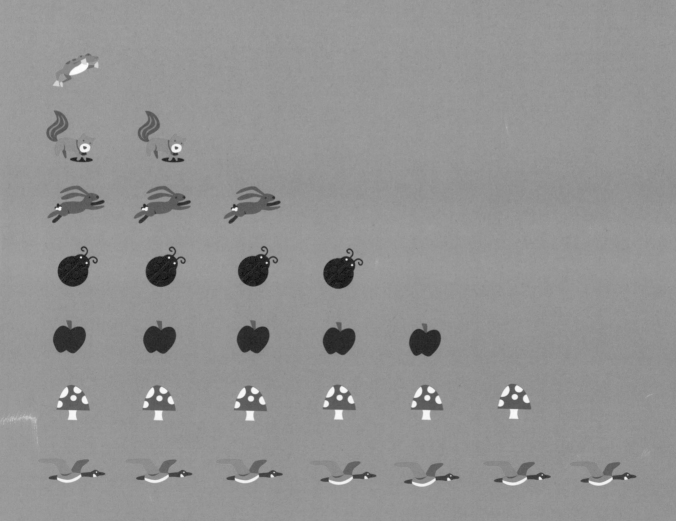

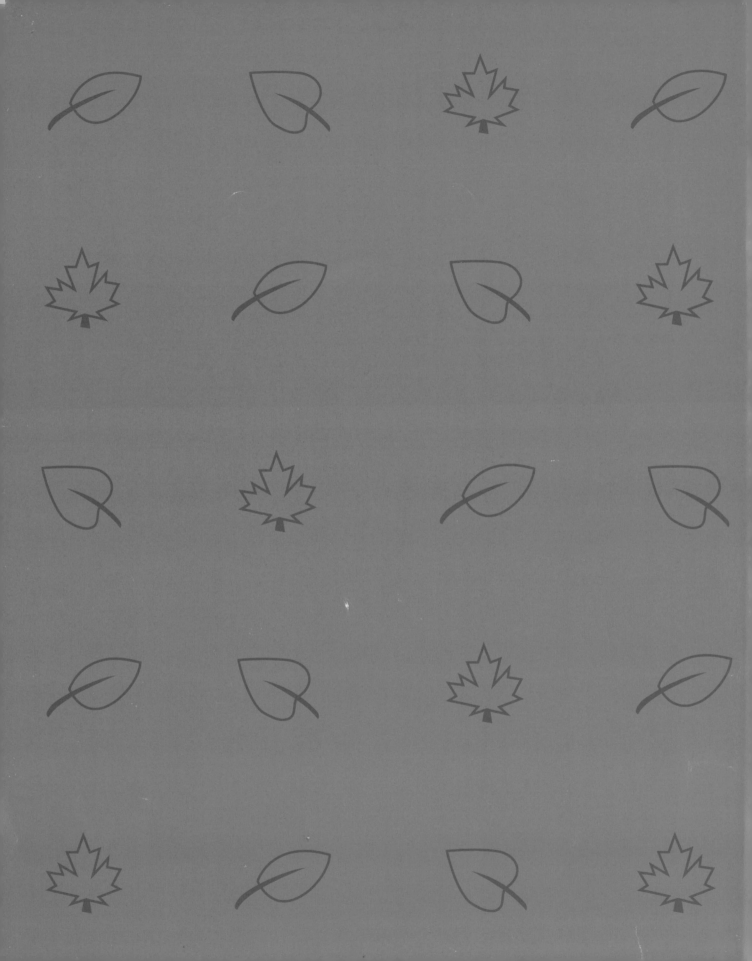